To my friend, Mrs. Katherine Goldman, who makes our world a better place by knitting for others and by teaching the next generation to knit so that they can do the same. —M.E.

For Sofia, who spells her name with an *F*.
And special thanks to the Purl Jam and Hudson Valley Sheep & Wool Company knitting groups for their kind and patient coaching. —G.B.K.

Text copyright © 2016 by Michelle Edwards. Jacket art and interior illustrations copyright © 2016 by G. Brian Karas. All rights reserved. Published in the United States by Schwartz & Wade Books, an imprint of Random House Children's Books, a division of Penguin Random House LLC, New York. Schwartz & Wade Books and the colophon are trademarks of Penguin Random House LLC. Visit us on the Web! randomhousekids.com ✿ Educators and librarians, for a variety of teaching tools, visit us at RHTeachersLibrarians.com ✿ *Library of Congress Cataloging-in-Publication Data* Names: Edwards, Michelle, author. | Karas, G. Brian, illustrator. Title: A hat for Mrs. Goldman : a story about knitting and love / by Michelle Edwards ; illustrated by G. Brian Karas. Description: First edition. | New York : Schwartz & Wade Books, [2016] |Summary: Sophia knits a special hat for her elderly neighbor and knitting teacher, Mrs. Goldman. Identifiers: LCCN 2015036747 | ISBN 978-0-553-49710-6 | ISBN 978-0-553-49711-3 (glb) | ISBN 978-0-553-49712-0 (ebk) Subjects: | CYAC: Knitting—Fiction. | Neighbors—Fiction. | Old age—Fiction. | Jews—United States—Fiction. | Mexican Americans—Fiction. Classification: LCC PZ7.E262 Hat 2016 | DDC [E]—dc23

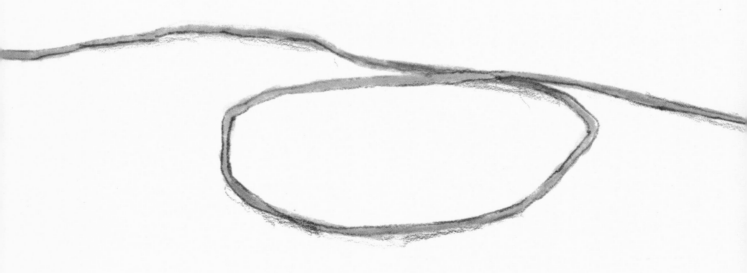

The text of this book is set in Deccan.
The illustrations were rendered in mixed media.
Book design by Rachael Cole
MANUFACTURED IN CHINA
2 4 6 8 10 9 7 5 3 1
First Edition

A Hat for Mrs. Goldman

A STORY ABOUT KNITTING and LOVE

by Michelle Edwards ❀ illustrated by G. Brian Karas

schwartz & wade books · new york

When Sophia was a tiny baby, Mrs. Goldman next
door knit her a tiny baby hat to keep her warm.

Now Sophia is big, and she makes the pom-poms for Mrs. Goldman's hats. Hats for the tiniest babies. Hats for small, medium, and large friends and neighbors. Mrs. Goldman taught her how.

"Keeping *keppies* warm is our *mitzvah*," says Mrs. Goldman, kissing the top of Sophia's head. "This is your keppie, and a mitzvah is a good deed."

Sophia and Mrs. Goldman bundle up to walk Mrs. Goldman's dog, Fifi. Winter is almost here. Fifi wears her dinosaur sweater. Sophia wears her fuzzy kitten hat and matching mittens.

Mrs. Goldman made them all.

An icy wind blows Mrs. Goldman's hair left and right.

It turns her ears pink.

"Where's your hat?" asks Sophia.

"I gave it to Mrs. Chen," she explains.

Mrs. Goldman's keppie must be cold, worries Sophia.

At home, Sophia thinks and worries again. Worries and thinks. Mrs. Goldman needs a hat. Who will knit one for her?

Not Mrs. Goldman. She's too busy knitting for everyone else.

Last year, Mrs. Goldman taught Sophia how to knit.

"I only like making pom-poms," decided Sophia after a few days.

"Knitting is hard. And it takes too long."

Now Sophia digs out the knitting bag Mrs. Goldman gave her. And the hat they started.

The stitches are straight and even. The soft wool smells like Mrs. Goldman's chicken soup.

Sophia holds the needles and tries to remember what to do. She drops one stitch. She drops another.

Still Sophia knits on. She wants to make Mrs. Goldman the most special hat in the world.

The next day when Sophia and
Mrs. Goldman walk Fifi, tiny fluffs
of snow fall on Mrs. Goldman's
head. Her ears are bright red.

Mrs. Goldman's keppie must
be very cold, frets Sophia.

Sophia knits after breakfast.

She knits after lunch.

She knits after dinner.

She even knits while Mama
reads her a bedtime story.

But Sophia doesn't knit when she is at Mrs. Goldman's
house. The hat is a surprise.

All week there's frost on the windows.
One day when they are walking Fifi,
Mrs. Goldman wraps Mr. Goldman's scarf
around her head like she's a mummy.

A fierce wind unwraps it and flings it up high.

Sophia jumps and grabs an end of the scarf.
Fifi nips at the other end.

Mrs. Goldman's keppie must be freezing, shivers Sophia.

Sophia knits and knits and knits. Faster and faster and faster.

Stitch by stitch. Row by row. Then Sophia sews.

At last, Mrs. Goldman's hat is done . . .

. . . sort of. The hat is lumpy and bumpy. There are holes where there shouldn't be holes.

It looks like a monster hat, thinks Sophia.

Sophia turns the hat over and around. Inside out. Mrs. Goldman's
hat should not be a monster hat that will scare Fifi.

Sophia opens the box of hats Mrs. Goldman made her. Each one is special, but they are all too small for Sophia now. And way too small for Mrs. Goldman.

Sophia looks in the hall closet. There are hats Mrs. Goldman made for Mama and Papa. She can't give her their hats! There is a scratchy old hat Sophia's abuela wore back in Mexico. Worse than Mr. Goldman's scarf.

Sophia thinks about Mrs. Goldman and the hats they make together. "Your pom-poms add beauty," Mrs. Goldman always tells her. "And that's a mitzvah, too."

Sophia feels her heart grow bigger and lighter, like a balloon.

She searches her room for red yarn. Red is Mrs. Goldman's favorite color. She gathers her scissors, her sewing needle, and her stack of index cards.

Sophia gets busy. Very busy.

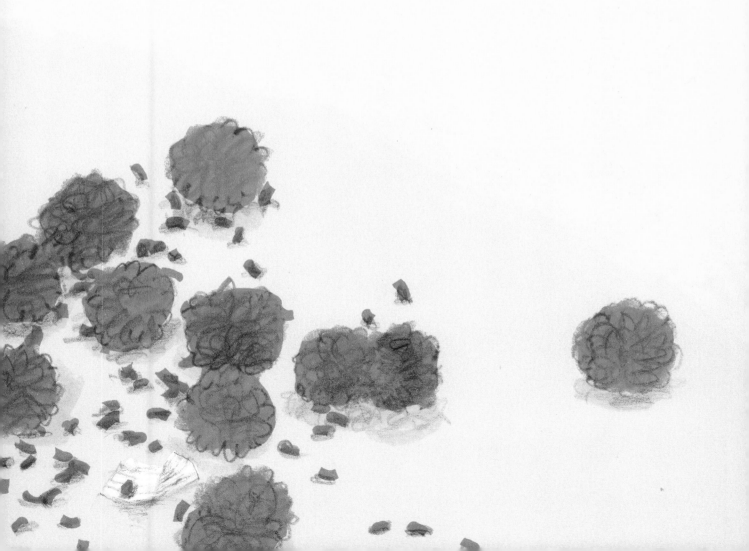

When Sophia is done, Mrs. Goldman's hat is the most special hat in the world.

Sophia rushes next door.

"Surprise!"

"For me?" asks Mrs. Goldman.

"For you," answers Sophia.

"It's a hat," she says.

"Of course it is!" exclaims Mrs. Goldman, and she hugs Sophia.

And then she cries.

"What's wrong?" asks Sophia. "Don't you like it?"

"I more than like it, I love it," declares Mrs. Goldman. "Gorgeous.
Like Mr. Goldman's rosebushes. And you know how I love his roses."

Mrs. Goldman kisses Sophia on top of her keppie.

"I made it all by myself," Sophia tells her.

"Amazing. And will you look at all these pom-poms? One, two, three, four . . . ," counts Mrs. Goldman. Sophia joins in.

There are twenty pom-poms on Mrs. Goldman's hat. Each one made with love.

She gently puts her hat on.

The next day, Sophia and Mrs. Goldman walk
Fifi. Fifi wears her dinosaur sweater. Sophia wears
her fuzzy kitten hat and matching mittens.

Mrs. Goldman wears her Sophia hat. Her keppie is
toasty warm. And that's a mitzvah.

HOW TO MAKE THE SOPHIA HAT

by Michelle Edwards and Theresa Gaffey

Sophia knit a hat for Mrs. Goldman; why don't you try to knit a hat, too? Here's the pattern.

SIZE: One size fits kid/adult

NEEDLES: Size 10 14-inch knitting needles

YARN: 1 ball of a chunky wool roving yarn,
like Lion Brand Alpine Wool

NOTIONS: Scissors, tape measure,
blunt-ended yarn needle, index card

GAUGE: Approximately 2.5 stitches per inch

HAT

- Cast on 25 stitches.
- Knit for 64 rows or 32 garter ridges. Lightly stretched, your knitting should measure about 22 inches wide and 9 inches tall.
- Bind off.
- Cut the yarn, leaving about a 30-inch tail.
- Fold the hat in half.
- Using the yarn needle and the tail of yarn, sew the cast-on edge to the bound-off edge.

- Using the rest of the yarn tail, gather the end stitches of each garter ridge along the top of the hat.
- Pull the yarn through gently and securely.
- Go through the end stitches again.
- Tie a knot and snip.
- Your hat is done!

If you want your hat to be just like the one Sophia made for Mrs. Goldman, you'll need to make some pom-poms.

POM-POMS

- Take an index card and fold it in two (along the shorter side).
- Halfway down the width of the card, cut a slit on either side, leaving about half an inch in the middle.
- Wrap your yarn 35 times around the middle of the card over the folded side.
- Cut the yarn from the ball.
- Cut another piece of yarn about 6 inches long and tie it through the cut slats.
- Cut the wrapped ends of yarn, remove the card, and trim the ends. Voilà!
- Using the yarn needle and a 6-inch length of yarn, sew the pom-pom onto the hat.
- Repeat!